ECHOES

Karina Evans

CONTENTS

ECHOES

Introduction

Why are you so comfortable with silence?

The words on the paper are just that: words. 'Echoes' projects those that we and others feel, observe, hear, but cannot always speak.

Echoes can be beautiful yet dangerous.

Anonymity absorbs them.

They can be whispered, shouted, absorbed, recalled, repressed, loved, hated, and forgotten. They are collected here for you to feel.

BUILDING

The building is old. It smells a little musty from every aspect, every corner. Dust settles on vertical windows and mould creeps into not-quite-right-angled corners. It creaks and sighs. The building is split into flats. Doors face forwards and sideways and backwards. Letters are put in holes. Fragile connective strands hang, taut in the air. Two, three, four, five, six flats. One is underneath. One is forgotten. Inhabited by silence, except the odd mouse you hear if you go to check the gas meter in the basement and put your ear to the letterbox. Maybe two mice. No point in one mouse squeaking alone; everyone needs someone to communicate with.

Mice in One. Listening. Inquisitive. Ears cocked, squeaking at the sighing.

A girl in Two. Trendy, pregnant, alone. Slamming doors indicate visitors. Doors slam and the building creaks. Ceilings shake. She shouts, "I don't love you anymore. I can do this alone." Sobbing. Kicking. Screaming.

Four people in Three. Closing their ears. Someone else will call the police. They drink wine and the children drink organic juice. Organic juice means they are cared for. The shop assistants look impressed as they buy it. They can get babysitters at the last minute, if they feel like taking some cocaine from the stash under the cupboard behind the curtain. Looking at the sea, sighing, pretending to be deaf.

A man in Four. He looks at porn. Sometimes porn he thinks he shouldn't look at. Legal, but too close to the bone. He is fifty-six. He is alone. He cries. When it's over, he angrily strips the sheets and feels guilty. He washes sheets. The washing machine rattles and the floors shake. The building sighs, but not in judgement. If he tilts his head inquisitively as he climbs the steps, he can see through the window of Two. He feels ashamed, alone, depressed, dirty. He tries not to look. It's not easy. One day she might thank him, if he sees something and breaks down the door. He thinks it is her he heard screaming.

A policeman and his wife in Five. They want a baby. At least, she does. She too looks through the window of Two, as she climbs the steps. She does not pretend not to; if Two can't be bothered to close her curtains, then she must want Five to see her caressing her swollen belly and cleaning broken glass off the floor. The only time

Five couldn't see Two was when Two's windows were boarded up. "Don't go down there," she had whined to her husband, the night she heard the faraway screaming and the shouting and the smashing. "Don't leave me, she can sort herself out. Fuck me." That always worked. He had fucked her, the headboard squeaking like mice, banging the wall, chipping the paint, slowly, reluctantly, and the building winced. He grunted but he didn't come. She didn't know he was fresh from fucking the probationer in the car.

The bloke visited Two again today. The restraining order didn't restrain him. He thinks it's pretty cool. Romeo and Juliet. Montagues and Capulets. Never let it be said that he is not a romantic. He knows he can be kind to her, if only she would STOP letting him go.

Six is up for rent. Restraining order keeps the bloke away. What a lovely view, through the freshly cleaned window. Not ideal for a family, too many stairs. Would the Asda delivery man carry the shopping up there? Ninety-eight steps.

Never get the wardrobe around those corners, but does it matter? What a lovely view.

One is not up for rent. Needs fixing and pest control. If it was up for rent, the bloke would move in. He used to live in Six; that's how he met her. Picking up post off the floor. Small talk. Big talk. Love, cohabitation, disaster. He is not allowed near her now, but he could break down the splintered, sharp door of One. Live with the mice and underneath Two. Staring at the ceiling staring at the floor. He would be able to hear if she had any visitors pinning her gently to the bed. The thought makes him angry. Nothing stopping him moving into One, though, is there? Squatting. Nobody will know. Six years and squatter's rights. Or five? Or four? He can't be sure. Word on the street goes round. Squatter's rights don't exist. A myth, or history, he can't remember. He can't Google because his smartphone screen is cracked. Dropped it, drunk, stamped on it. Voice activated dialling works if he depresses the Home button for long enough and shouts in an accent. That's how he contacts her. Sometimes he plays a game. Ring. Ring ring. "Hello?" Hang up. Ring. Ring ring. "Hello?" Hang up. Once, he did this four times in a row. But now she knows, because he had spoken. He still phones, she cowers, the room shrinks, nobody answers.

Now it is summer. It is meant to be, but the weather makes everyone talk. They laugh. They say, "Bloody British weather," shrug off their kagouls and dry jeans on radiators. The building swells and shrinks, and the smell of warm washing powder emanates from radiators in every flat, except One and Two. One can't get the gas connected. Or the electricity. He washes in warm water at the sports centre, before the swimmers come in. He gets his post sent to Mum's and collects it once a week. She doesn't mind if he signs on from her address. She will do anything to make him happy. She buys him food and cries when he says she can't visit him. "But I'll visit you, Mum. You don't need to see my little flat." Casseroles and chocolate cake and cups of tea. He doesn't drink anymore, which is a relief. Buys his coke from organic guy in Three. When he was little, he told his Mum he wanted to go away to live with his Dad. His Dad was cool; he wore jeans and waistcoats and smoked joints. His Mum bought him a bike and some fags, so he stayed.

Two can't afford to keep putting the heating on. She is saving money for the baby. Eight days left and she has a hundred and eighteen pounds. It's cold, despite the month. She lives in one room with one blanket. The room feels larger when it's cold, and the draughts rattle her through the window that looks out onto the steps. She plans that when the baby is born, the baby called Eva or Sonny, she will put the heating on all day if its skin feels cold. She will put it in its Moses basket, feet at the end so it doesn't wriggle under the blanket. On its back. Forehead thermometer every two hours, just in case. When its skin heats the top end of the green section on the thermometer, the heating will go off. Nobody will judge her. She is only seventeen, but she will bathe her baby twice a day.

She doesn't need a pram. She wants the baby close to her skin. Under a jumper, or in a sling, so she can see it breathing. Feel it breathing. She can't understand why people face babies away from them. Strangers coming at them, smiling, gap-toothed, staring. Baby needs Mummy's face and Mummy's heart.

Five are not all at home. He went to work. She doesn't know that he doesn't work anymore. Leaves in his white shirt and black trousers, returns in his white shirt and black trousers. He says he has a locker at work. Epaulettes, hat and jacket in it. Safe. A week now. He told her he is doing day shifts this week. Ten till six. What happens next week when he is meant to be working nights? He was suspended on full pay, investigation pending. Pretended he was on leave. Six weeks it took. After two weeks, he told her he was stressed. Took his sandwiches to the park when he said he was at the doctor's getting signed off. He couldn't pretend to be stressed forever, even though he was. Stressed because he was not stressed. Soon she will notice they can't afford anything. She will notice the letters down the back of the fridge, turning at the corners, dried and pointed, grey with damp from the wall. Creeping and contaminated. Name and address in black. Red lines poking under the envelope window. FINAL DEMAND. The water will go and the electricity will go and her dream will go. All because he got caught fucking the probationer in the car.

Right now, he is eating his sandwiches on a park bench. He is under a raincloud. It's a shame that his favourite view is the sea; he can't eat his sandwiches by the sea. She will peer from the window and there he will be and the game will be over. He hasn't considered the local press. They jump on the police, ever since the police failed to catch the man who tried to touch up children in the play park. The police are shit. Still on the run. The police are fucked. Fucking paedo. The police are corrupt. Look at this one! He fucked a probationer in a police car. Spunk on the seats. Fired. Eating sandwiches, staring unblinkingly at his second favourite view. Water gone. Electricity gone. Life gone.

Three are out. Not all of them. The adults are out. They'll be back by nine. Their niece will babysit. Sixteen. She will text her boyfriend and tell him that she wishes she was with him instead. She will eat biscuits while she texts him filth. She will stare at the wall while thinking of adjectives. She will notice the painted cracks they thought had been hidden.

The adults went out because they wanted a meal.

A silent meal. Their food is piled high, garnished with something that can't be eaten. No noise from the mouths of babes. Babes who climb from their beds wanting a cuddle. Time thieves. Independence thieves. Shoo them back. If only we had a nanny. A nanny in the daytime to show them pebbles from the beach and get paint on her skirt. A nanny at night to let the adults have their beauty sleep. Ugly inside. Look at the children's beautiful faces. Let his hair grow. Buy him red trousers. She can wear tights and a swishy skirt and people will coo. They are so beautiful. So beautiful. So demanding.

It's the next day. Two hadn't noticed him watching. Didn't know he had been watching for a week. Planning a cliché. "If I can't, no-one can.". But she had felt a bit on edge. Put it down to tiredness. Baby had been heavy and pressing down on her pelvis, making her ache. Head engaged, she couldn't sleep. Excitement and weariness. When she had opened the door, at ten past ten in the morning, she expected the postman. Not the bloke. The last thing she expected was to be stabbed.

Five had seen him watching her. The bloke. Five had seen the bloke three or four times in the same week. Emerging from the basement, feral. Unkempt. Weeds from the ground staining his white shoes, tainting a blank canvas. Anger in his walk. Disjointed hips, perhaps. Side to side to side, swinging shoulders, chin in the air. Too big for his boots, the little runt. Today, sunny-at-last today, Five saw him again. Marching with purpose. His police nose twitched, then he remembered he had to pretend to go to work. None of his business, right? He pretended he had no time. Sandwiches had to be eaten. Swans and pigeons waiting for crumbs. Looking. He could see glistening in a waistband. Reflecting. Could be a belt, sun glistening on a belt. But that walk. That bloke. That watching. A knife? Five walked to the park.

The adults in Three nursed hangovers. They had been late back last night, bunged the niece an extra twenty, like that made it ok. This morning the beautiful children made noise and the adults held hands over ears. She looked at the beautiful children, then looked out the window. Saw the window frame first, spotted with mould, taking over. She saw the bloke she had seen before. The bloke who had made Two scream. She rolled her eyes. Focused again. He was walking, swinging his arms. She saw his hand, his hand, his hand, his hand, a knife. Saw a knife. No. He wouldn't. Probably visiting. Unpacking baby stuff. Opening boxes. She suppressed her panic.

Four feels ashamed, dirty, unworthy, loathed, unloved, detested, marginalised, ostracised. He is a bad man. Still, that doesn't stop him looking through the window of Two when he comes back from the shop. He had seen running, a man running. Not a jogger. Perhaps a crime. It ties together when he sees her lying there. Holding her stomach. Eyes open. Terror. Fright. Fear. Hatred. Panic. Love. Blood. He has his keys. He opens the first door. It lets him in. Barges through the second door, which relents on the third attempt. Stems the flow of blood. Whispers words. Comforting words. Strokes her head. It will be ok, yes. The baby will be ok, yes. Don't worry, my love. Don't worry. Fumbling fingers, stemming blood, dialling for help, stemming blood, waiting, waiting, waiting.

Sirens and voices and machines.

Five is in the park. His wife is at home. He doesn't know she finds out today. She sees the police, police she knows. Scene guard. She's part of the police family, you see. Been to Christmas parties, flirted with Inspectors, worn glittery dresses and gold boleros. She is pleased to see them. Inquisitive. Is someone else's life ruined, she asks. I can't say, they say. Bad news about your husband, my love. You still together. Yes, yes, we are. You're a better woman than I am, Mrs. Why is that, then. No philandering man would ever put his slippers under my bed again, certainly not, no. A probationer too. A shame. Lost his career and hers too.

I'm so sorry.

They stemmed the blood, cut out the baby, heard it cry, rested it on her. She is prone, unconscious, but they think she will stay alive. They will look after her. Her mother will travel down, break the silence, take her back home. She will add Four on Facebook and say thank you when she feels better. A knife in the gut is never not going to hurt. It still twists, but she is full of hearts and flowers and her soul sings as she hears crying in her sleep.

TEASPOONS AND PERFECTION

You think she's ok, then you lean in, observe the black crayon scribbles under her eyes and the sunset streaks across her cheeks. Make-up hides it, almost enough. She spins on her heel and walks towards the sea, wind whipping her hair around and up and down, pointing at the skies, at hell, at the options. She is wondering, the same as you. Wondering and wandering in a world which can't be perfect. You discuss books together: The Kite Runner, Anne Frank's Diary...you both know it could be worse.

You're safe in your life, in your lives. The shopping gets delivered by a man in a van. The van is themed. A vegetable, usually. You have a list of your favourite vans. Your furniture is fashionably old: battered and not black ash. Floral patterns might get replaced when geometric comes back. You laugh about stuff. A lot. There's a lot of laughing. You breathe life into each other, talk into each other's mouths. But you both dwell on the decisions you can't make. And when you can't make them you ask the universe, but expect the universe not to judge.

Why is she worrying? Why didn't she sleep? She didn't sleep because you can't agree on everything. And you think of the war on terror and the concentration camps, and she thinks of these too. You both feel small. You can march on through your lives, leaving unmade decisions behind, because, after a while, the Best Before date runs out and the choices disappear. Inaction. Where do they go, unmade decisions, you wonder. With teaspoons and odd socks and the mundane memories that are not good enough, bad enough or dramatic enough. Recycled and reborn. And although it's imperfect, you know that it's closer to perfect than it could be.

SHE WENT TO HIS FUNERAL, YOU KNOW

Jessica Louise Bennett, aged 21 years and zero days

February 2017

She walks.

If she thinks about it deeply, she can force out a tear. If she concentrates, squeezing her eyes closed as tight as she can until she sees black, then red, then white, she can force two. She likes to think that there's one for her mum and one for herself. But the guy who used to be her father, no, no, he deserves none.

She walks.

He cursed the family, she thinks. A voodoo doll picnic with a masochistic torturer. She had denied the voice in her head so far, thinking that if she didn't

15

step out in front of the car, if she didn't throw herself from the top of the building, if she didn't go from shop to shop, stocking up on paracetamol, forcing them down her gagging throat as her body tried to reject them, if she didn't do any of that, then maybe she could beat it.

She walks.

There's a series of films about a bunch of teens who are destined to die and, no matter what they do, how many times they cheat death, their destiny remains the same. The agony is prolonged, but death still chases them. The lives they live are examples of agony, of desperation, of battles, of pain. But still they carry on, the grim reaper on their backs — a heavy weight in a survivalist's backpack.

The only reason Jessica is alive today is because she has been refusing to die.

She walks.

It's her birthday today, and she expected that it would be just like any other day, that she would wake, stretch her arms in the air, feel the space above her, next to her; a gap beside her where, one day, she always imagined somebody would want to lie beside her. But a new idea pushed itself to the front of her mind, and she knew it was time.

She walks.

She went to his funeral, you know, they whispered. That guy who broke her arm, who locked her in a cupboard, who beat her mum, who killed himself in prison; she watched from the back, they frowned.

She was fourteen then and she had held anger between her teeth, biting down to suppress it. She bit so hard a molar had cracked and she runs her tongue along it now, feeling the comforting sharp edge threatening to cut her. Ashes to ashes, they had said as she held her own hands until the bones screamed at her to just quit, wringing her fingers to stop them ripping the lid from the coffin to claw at the decaying face inside. The face that turned to ashes, the ashes in a jar in a corner of a cupboard in her life.

She walks.

Her life was ok on paper, from fourteen upwards. But isn't it the shit before that shapes us, that forms our happiness? Isn't it childhood that sets the salt dough of our minds; trapping thoughts and emotional patterns? Aren't the most important years the ones in which you are taught about love, about being held, about feeling as though you are adored? It isn't that bit when, at fourteen, your father suspends his bodyweight from a belt in a prison cell, cutting off the oxygen to his broken brain, snapping his neck, forcing his tongue from his mouth, a grotesque caricature of the man the prison guard had seen on his last check fifty-nine minutes beforehand.

She walks.

Time only ticks if you put the battery in the right way, her grandfather had told her; her dear, dear Pops. Concentrate on the positive end of the battery, he showed her, the negative fits easily; it's the positive you need to work on.

She walks.

Anonymous people stream past her; tourists whose day jobs are as bankers, nurses, shop assistants. There are dads, mums, aunts, daughters, people with penthouse apartments, people with seven children in tiny homes, children, teenagers, the poor, the rich, the distracted. They all hold their existences so closely to their chests, as though if they share — a smile, a nod — their lives will no longer be special. Among these blurred outlines are people who have loved, who have climbed towers of pain and stayed at the top, people who hate, people who lash out, who scare, who feel powerful. There are people who shrink away from touch, people who run towards it, people who drink, people who need to be held. And then there's Jessica, with weight on her shoulders.

She walks, she stops, she looks down. She has arrived.

She holds her arms out and breathes in, inhaling the day. She tilts her head back, feeling the pull on her throat, and closes her eyes; writers always say you feel the warmth of the sun when you do this, but they don't mention that when the sun isn't out and the sky is grey that the grey gets inside you. She thinks of her mum, so beaten so broken, and of her dad, so mistaken so shattered, and for the first time she cries for him, for the man who didn't know how to stop, who left a burning residue behind, who took his own life after ruining so many. She cries as she imagines leaning forward, and she reckons that she would still be crying five slow free seconds later when she hit the rocks at the bottom.

The rucksack strap has slipped from her shoulders and she contorts her arm through it, releasing its hold. She opens the bag; she removes the weight.

She holds him in her fingertips, but can't bring herself to tighten her fingers, to touch him, to feel his coolness inside her hands. She looks over the cliff that her mum and dad had held so close in their lives. A happier day, a happier week, a holiday of forgiveness, of repenting, of false declarations of fresh starts. And Jessica lifts the lid off the urn that she has held so far away from herself, and she watches as her father gets carried away on the wind.

CORROSION

She finds it hard to describe, that love she never had. The best friend that wasn't, no endless cups of tea, no laughing, no oh, I simply-have-to-tell-my-mum.
Sit down, deep breaths, tell me how you feel.

NOTES

She says that when she hunted for and found the strings that had been cut, nobody stared in wonder, with tears in their eyes. Nobody said, well let's see you then, you look like me, and made her twirl in front of them. Nobody said I'm sorry. She says she realised that when the strings are cut, you crumple alone.

She tells me she went back home, to the home that had chosen her, and she hoped for arms to pull her to her feet. But she found an angry face, a pointing finger, and she had to swim the stream of guilt.

She sees how special a constructed bond can be, and she feels a cog begin to move. Its rusted wheel clanks and scrapes, carrying memories, remnants of things-that-shouldn't-have-been-said-or-done.

So why do you think she chose you, I ask.

she needed to fill a hole that had appeared, she replies. But I wasn't big enough; I simply wasn't big enough.

and who pulled you to your feet, I ask her.

what nobody realises when you are lying in a heap on the floor, she says, is that when you eventually look up, all you can see is light.

NINE SECONDS
OF ANONYMITY

He shuffles along, his mind as heavily laden as the stormy clouds above him. Each step he takes is wearier than the last, and, at times, he thinks he will not make it. He is struggling, yet persevering; he needs to reach his destination; it is where he belongs. As he walks, he observes. He examines the buildings full of memories, and the gutters full of mistakes. His feet are bare inside his worn-down leather shoes, they are slipping in sweat created by the stifling, stormy atmosphere. In the house to his left, a faceless woman cradles a newborn baby. A male looks over her shoulder to peer at the crinkled face of his son and heir. Seconds later, they all disappear from sight. He knows they will never be that happy again.

He looks ahead. He stops. The window of a pub displays its clientele. A man, aged approximately thirty-five, is standing at the bar. The man is clearly drunk; he is leaning against the bar for support, fumbling with some change, needing another pint. Grabbing onto his leg is a small boy. Tears roll down the boy's cheeks. The boy needs attention. The boy is saying something important. He knows that the boy wants to be picked up and held. He knows the boy wants to be listened to.

His feet are aching, and his stomach is churning. He shuffles onwards, towards his destination, his home: his mecca. The walk feels like it is taking hours, but he can sense that the length is deceptive, and the journey poignant in its slow motion.

A teenage boy cycling towards him at high speed startles him. He sidesteps to avoid collision, and winces as the boy hurls a string of expletives in his general direction. He curses the reckless lack of respect of the youth of today, as he bends to adjust a lace that is sitting uncomfortably inside his shoe. As he straightens, he tries to view himself in the glass of a shop window, but his focus is blurry, and all he can see are the people inside the premises. The shop is a model shop, selling plastic aeroplanes and cars, all sitting neatly in their boxes, until an enthusiast deems it essential to purchase and lovingly nurture them to life. A scruffy-looking man in his mid-twenties is inside the shop, and he watches with disgust as he picks up a tube of model glue to work inside his coat sleeve, until obscured from the view of the shopkeepers. He briefly ponders why it is necessary to steal such an item, as surely its value is negligible, and hardly worth a stint in the cells. He suspects the man will use it to get high. He shakes his head, and moves on.

He has arrived at a cul-de-sac, decorated by young trees and bushes with their best years ahead of them. He bends down to pick a rose, but cannot feel its silky petals between his sweaty thumb and forefinger. He hears a scream, and looks up to see a partially opened window, a female face pressed against it. A man is standing behind her, pummelling blows upon her broken body, shouting above her screams. He can see blood and he can see tears, but what can he do? He can do nothing, it is too late.

He walks on, despite his aching feet, and sees a church. It is magnificent, regardless of its impoverished location. He peers through the arched doors, and notices an elderly lady sitting on a pew at the back. She is alone. He steps gently inside the church, and listens as the lady softly utters a prayer, a prayer of salvation for a loved son who has turned bad. He feels like holding her, holding the anonymous woman who has loved so utterly deeply and unconditionally, yet achieved nothing but hate. The lady turns, and he is shocked to see bruises upon her soft face. Painful darkness, disappearing between the deep lines of what could have been a beautiful life.

He is shocked, and stumbles back towards the doors of the church, reaching forwards for support as he feels nausea welling inside him. Through the darkness in front of his eyes, he can see a beautiful horizon, but this cannot stop him vomiting violently on the tiled floor at the entrance of the church. He wipes his mouth, and urges himself onwards. He must keep walking, for his destination is looming. His stamina is waning, but he calls upon his inner strength to move himself onwards. There is no one left to support him, nobody to show him the way, he needs to find the right path on his own.

There is a young woman heading towards him on the footpath. The woman is approximately twenty years old, and simply stunning in an understated way. Her blonde hair is tied in an almost child-like ponytail, and she bounces slightly as she listens to music through foam-covered headphones. As if from a clichéd nowhere, a man appears behind her. The man looks familiar; the anger on his face is proverbial of a mugger, a rapist, a murderer, or perhaps all three. The woman screams as he pushes her to the floor and rips a purse from her pocket. The sky is turning blacker by the second, and he feels its ominous presence crushing him. He is as powerless as she is, and the words he needs to shout to stop the brutal attack are stuck in his dry throat as he cowers behind a bush. He silently and helplessly watches the dying woman as she attempts to fight off her attacker. This is the last fight of her short life, it is a fight against a man almost twice her size, a fight she cannot win. He knows that her lifeless body will remain in that exact position until a passer-by happens upon her later in the day. To that passer-by, it will seem a merciless killing, but he knows that she paid the ultimate price in an exhibition of power and control. The man who killed her feels like God right now, and he will feel like God until he is scorned for his actions.

He notices a glove on the ground, carelessly dropped by the attacker, and he tuts his disapproval as he knows that this innocuous item will be the killer's downfall, the last downfall of many.

The sky suddenly lightens, as the storm clouds part to reveal a beautiful sun. The darkness has lifted, and the light is welcoming and warm.

Clusters of buildings are ahead of him, surrounded by a high wire fence. The irony is not lost on him, as he considers that the brutal crime was committed just metres from a prison. He can hear joviality, which strikes him as odd. Joviality in the face of oppression does not sit well with him. He cannot see them, but he knows that amongst them is at least one who does not laugh, who does not cry, who does not wish to exist anymore. There is one who knows that to repent for his sins, he must die. There is one man inside the prison block who is slashing at his wrists, because the overdose did not work. That man is he; I am that man. This has been my life: these have been my memories, my mistakes, and my countless sins. This has been my journey, and now I must leave. The nine second flash of life before the darkness of my death is complete. This is my destination.

LONG RING, NO REPLY – DEATH OF THE FINEST

It's ok
It's ok because
It's ok because he
It's ok because he will
It's ok because he will answer
It's ok because he will answer for me
He will answer for me

Ring. No answer

He will answer for me

Ring
Again

No answer
Again, no answer

Again

Ring again
Ring again; no
answer

Answer
Answer
Answer

No Answer

Long ring, no reply

SECOND SIN

Yesterday:

Bless me Father, for I have sinned

Homework: write a poem about something you regret

Like a present

waiting to be opened

Like a past

Expecting...

to be erased

It exists

if only to be regretted

A truth

that nobody knows

If I could take my mistakes

and draw them again,

would I compromise

and forget...

my best sin?

A work

awaiting completion

The conclusion

of a heart

That began beating

I didn't think

I didn't know

Education?

A sin

A rhyme

An end

With a forgettable beginning.

Today:

Molly holds the rosary beads tightly in her hand, feeling the warm, fleece lining of her jacket pocket encasing her cold hand. She needs to count her sins, but having had a lot on her mind lately, she has neglected to bring her prayer beads. For a familiar moment, she feels like a fake: looking for Him, not in His house, but in an ordinary street with ordinary people and ordinary buildings. A fraud. That's what her mother told her last night, when the realisation had set in.

'A good Catholic girl, Molly. That's what you are meant to be, that's who we raised you to be.'

Molly struggles with this, she is no longer a good Catholic girl, and is unsure whether she ever has been.

'When did you forget this? How could you forget this? When did you become this person?'

Molly had then pulled her baggy jumper tightly around her stomach, inducing an unprecedented rage in her mother.

'Look at yourself! You are a FRAUD, pretending to be someone you are not, hiding under those hideous clothes!'

Molly knew her mother well, and knew that in different circumstances she may have laughed, even been impressed, at Molly's current talent for disguise. She understood that her mother had to be angry, but all she really wanted was for her to say that everything would be alright. A soothing stroke of the hair and a chocolate biscuit, and everything would be okay.

'You deserve more...we deserve more. We told you to forget the boys, avoid the sins. Concentrate on Him, we said, for He has the answers; He is the guiding light. A GOOD CATHOLIC GIRL, THAT IS WHO YOU ARE MEANT TO BE.'

Molly is now a statistic, which she feels is no less fraudulent than scrubbing her cheeks until they sting, donning a pretty frock, and pretending to believe something that she cannot see. Molly's school friends – 'they are not true friends, they are leading you astray,'– have always mocked her mother, mocked her father, mocked her faith. This is why

Molly sinned that evening. She sinned so that she would fit in, be one of them, and be far less than a compromise. This is why Molly is here now, right now, clutching plastic beads from a fashion store.

Does it matter?

It is another compromise. The rosary beads in her pocket, they aren't real, but she thinks she should probably use them to guide her.

Hail Mary.

Two sins, at the last count. The first being the stolen moment in the woods with Simon after the school disco, seventeen weeks ago. Simon is a popular boy, and Molly was understandably flattered that he wanted to spend some time with her. Molly had never before imagined the consequence of time. She would, in all likelihood, still be flattered if Simon continued to want to spend time with her, but now time means nothing to him; he points and he laughs and he mocks along with the rest of them. Molly smiles, she likes to smile through adversity, and she knows that the secret – his secret – that ticks away inside her, will soon wipe that smug grin from his face. Molly places her hand on her stomach. Life. A life that began in a damp wood: a life moulded with fumbling hands, a beautiful beginning, a perfect being, made by amateurs, in a shocking showcase of beginners' luck.

If faith had allowed them, Molly is sure her incensed parents would have marched her to a clinic to remove the sin from sight and from memory. But this had not been the case. Through whispers and through anger Molly had felt a hazy blur of burdened love emanating from them. A weakness growing stronger through misfortune. They were furious, but they were forced to accept, forced to forgive and forced to support.

'A child?' Your child?'

Your grandchild.

Molly feels for the beads in her pocket, and counts down to bead number two, closing her eyes in concentration. She does not want anyone to see. She does not want anyone to mock. She does not want anyone to judge. She does not want to care.

Errare humanum est

To err is human

Molly has been forced to count her sins on many occasions, but this time – the time she wants and needs to – she cannot bring herself to do it. Molly wonders why and she looks towards the sky, searching for an answer. He is there, this is what they say. He is everywhere, He is all encompassing, therefore it matters not where she looks.

Forgive

Judge

Retribution

Yet, He does not give her an answer, nor does He comfort her. Molly inhales deeply on the cigarette she is holding in her free hand, and strolls – with a confidence she cannot bring herself to feel – towards the ashtray. Another sin to add to the list, she thinks with a smug bitterness. A sin that is bad for the life inside her, bad for the beating heart. Molly just wants to be accepted. Molly just wants to be happy. Pure, simple, unadulterated happiness, the thought of which makes her feel sorry for herself. Molly occasionally allows herself the indulgence of emotion, and now she feels another deep in her stomach, twisting, hurting, punishing her. Guilt. Guilt for the sin, guilt for the cigarette, guilt for the compromise and guilt for being unable to ask forgiveness for any of them. Molly's knees tremble as a wave of nausea washes over her, and she sinks to the ground, holding her head in her hands. It is nearly tea-time, and she is sure that despite her failings, her parents will want her back for her meal. Molly struggles to her feet, holding her stomach, holding on to the precious life that will love her forever. It is a sin for which she cannot possibly ask for forgiveness, because it is a sin that she will never regret.

Molly's second sin was another compromise: a struggle between being a Good Catholic Girl and being part of the crowd that had grown to occasionally tolerate her, despite her obvious faults. Molly again fumbles in her pocket for the beads and, holding them tightly, rises to her feet to pay for the second sin. She walks slowly back to-

KARINA EVANS

wards the doors, proudly thrusting out her growing stomach that she has deliberately encased in a
tight, white T-shirt. She feels them looking, feels
them judging her, but now she does not care, for she
can only ever truly be judged by Him, and He is nowhere to be seen.

'Babies having babies,' she hears someone mutter as
she walks past them.

A walk of shame.

Molly laughs as tears well in her eyes: another
contrast, another compromise, but she walks on,
tasting the bitterness of the cigarette she has just
smoked, mingling with the sourness of guilt. In
front of her is a row of shops and Molly wishes that
she had some money to spend; she wants to buy
something for her baby. She would buy a dummy,
or a rattle or a tiny, knitted pair of bootees. She
just wants to make the fluttering real, solid and un-
changeable. Molly shakes her head to bring herself
back to the matter in hand, the baby is moving and
willing her on. This is the beginning, a new beginning, a new start that she will never regret. Molly
is a huge fan of irony, and the humour of this situ-
ation is not lost on her. She raises her chin defiantly
and walks back into the shop in which she had
been ten minutes ago. Time goes so slowly when
you are looking for something. She finally reaches
the counter, and spots a friendly looking sales as-
sistant, wearing a badge that proclaims her name

is Jennifer. Jennifer makes her way over to Molly, fleetingly taking notice of her rounded stomach.

'Can I help you?' Jennifer asks softly.

'Yes, I think you can. I stole these, you see, and I thought I should return them. They don't seem to work anyway.'

'That's irony, eh? Did they come in useful?'

'I don't think I need to atone for this, you know. This is my Best Sin.'

Bless me Father, for I have sinned.

I believe

in something worth believing

My life

is waiting to be born

I regret

nothing worth regretting

I waste no time

on the consequence

of a mistake that means everything

Then and now

time is drawn,

in black,

upon white paper.

Indelible.

Accept me Father,

Accept me for me.

I forgive you Father
I thank you for this:
My best sin.

DENSITY

Did we ever speak of my broken heart?
How I tiptoed amid the smell of sleep
And while time ticked, I found the truth
Glowing silently, piercing pieces of heavy hearts.

I wrote a poem of perfection.
Remember.
Moonlight and reflection.
It stung your eyes because you loved me so,
how did you say goodbye, my darling?
With a soft sound and tenderness?
A lover far away
while another densely lingers.

                                    And words.
                        Words will start a war,
            or finish the fight, which quietly flourished
And hearts can be held, when beating out of time,

but dates, times and memories,
they stop me.

Dead.

PAST PERFECT

If she knew she was going to die now, she'd have lived more carefully. Lived more cynically, perhaps. More precisely. She'd have loved more, hated more, taken more. She's here now though, right here, right now, exhaling stolen breaths left carelessly by an imprecise bullet. Here she is. Here she is, dying.

Easy, isn't it, to look back on your life when you are no longer in it, when you are distanced and devoid?

Easy, isn't it, to look at the film being played and will yourself to run faster, punch harder, hug tighter, say words that are stuck in your throat? Easy.

Last thing that happens in life is the playback. It's a life, an actual life. Your life. You are watching it, behind your dying eyes, but it's tactile and tangible. You smell the grass, touch the sea. But not the people. Try as you might to pick yourself up – like the little man on online maps – and move yourself along ten metres, you can't. Try as you might, you can't.

You can't change anything, because it's happened. The purpose of it is punishment, presumably. Dying isn't hurting, but life on a fucking reel smarts. I'd rather feel the pain of the bullet wedged in my throat, feel the pain of my organs working too hard, trying to keep me alive. Deciding which one should stop working, which is the least important. Shut down her kidneys she probably needs her heart more shut down her heart she probably needs her brain more shut down her brain.

It could be minutes or hours or days, it's all so slow. Not hearing voices, because later I see them. Third person, through another's eyes. A book, a tome, from beginning to end.

It all goes backwards, rewinds, not slow enough to filter anything, to grasp where it went wrong, but slow enough to recognise faces. The volume is up, everyone is screeching, screaming. Suddenly, it halts, it bounces, and that's me, there's a light. Born into the right family. It's going quite quickly now, born, home, growing, feeding, laughing, falling, crying, swimming. Pauses on another face. Rewind. Shows the face again, this is hard work. I recognise my brother. Looks like a waster, even as an eight-year-old.

Ever wondered if you would kill a killer if you had met them as a child?

Now I want to reach in, grab Mark's neck and squeeze the ugly life from him as he pedals his beautiful little blue bicycle.

I see me. I am six. It's going quicker now.

Faster faster faster.

Mark is ten and I am eight. He pushes me off the swing.

Oh, boys, what are they like? Don't worry though, because when you need him most he'll come through. He's your big brother, kiddo.

Except the playback shows that I look into his eyes and recoil and I remember that his eyes were matte and sharp even then. I knew as an eight year-old that Mark, my big brother, was not my protector.

Forward, but more slowly. Mum drinking, Dad ignoring, sometimes shouting, telling Mark he is not a real boy, he is not strong, he is a weed and he is weak, and nobody seeing that fourteen-year-old Mark is quiet and pale and things have disappeared.

Mark gets quieter and paler as the playback goes on. He is still taking things that aren't his and he goes out at night. I'm still at school and I know my grammar, I can do equations without a calculator, but Mark bunked off and left, college wouldn't take him, so he bums around. Sixty quid a week he gets. Sixty quid's worth of cash that goes I don't know where. I know now but it wasn't my place to know then, and my parents were blind or stupid or ignorant. He takes the key from the bowl on the sideboard and he sneaks out the front door at midnight. He is seventeen. I am fifteen. He is in a gang of sorts. Smoking, he stinks of smoke; drinking, he stinks of booze; taking drugs, he stinks of nothing; but pupils always bigger than his eyes or more recently so small that I can't see them. But it's ok because he causes no problems. I watch myself following him one night. It's the night he went out earlier than usual; parents out at the pictures, rekindling and fixing, taking in a film and eating popcorn, Dad probably copping a feel and Mum slapping his hand away, whilst Mark takes the key and walks the streets. He gets in a car, a red car, and they put the music on so loud that my stomach dances. I see a flame. They are smoking. Sighing, I turn away, but a car door opens and voices mumble and a car door slams and someone screams and I turn back. Mark is out the car and he is punching with both fists. It's a girl. Never seen her before. Double my age, perhaps. Pretty but thin. I knew this but I hadn't remembered until now. He is punching her and I don't know why and I don't know what to do.

Older brothers protect sisters, but not this one. I ask him when he gets home, why did you punch the girl, is she ok? **Why did you follow me, you little fucking bitch?** Why? **She had my gear,** what gear, **my drugs,** what drugs, **I gave her money, money to make my head spin, money to make me forget the arguments and Dad forcing himself on Mum, I heard that, you know, one night, so I gave the girl some money for gear, the gear, and she lost it.** Mark cries. I watch myself feeling sorry for him and I want to pick myself up and move myself away, knowing what I know now. But I hug him tighter and he probably feels like he has got me on side.

And then it gets slower. My parents split. Dad moves one hundred and seven miles away, says he **loves** Mum too much not to be with her, he can't **see** her, he can't **speak** to her, we **remind** him of her and **no,**

no,

no,

no,

he won't give her any money, he just needs to **forget** his abject **misery**, he has no children, as far as he is concerned. He had held us, in past perfect tense, looking at us lovingly, but no, he does not want to **remember** us.

I am watching but I don't want to. Mark is nineteen, I am seventeen. Mark is even paler and thinner and his jeans hang down below his hips and his body is unclean, his mind too. There are charcoal smudges under his eyes and he has lost some teeth to methadone. He still takes the methadone on top. He is cutting down though, he tells me, but he needs to be away from Mum to do it properly, away from the crying and the sleeping and the denials of love. He is moving out to live with a friend at a hostel, don't try to find him, look after Mum, ok? I have a job at a shop, selling tat to tourists. Beach balls, windbreaks – despite the rain they buy them. They get sand in their faces but it doesn't matter, not on holiday. I listen to Mark, I leave the job, it only pays six quid an hour anyway and Mum has money from the limp she got when she fell down the stairs. A transient disability and now she has a permanent career. I can't not watch, I don't want to watch; I know what happens next; I know what happened two days later. On this morning, this sunny morning, I have to find Mark because something terrible happened and I can't see Mark because he has walked away, but what I CAN see is my mother lying on the floor with vomit under her head, drying around her mouth and her skin is grey and I am pumping her chest and breathing my clean sweet air into her stinking mouth and dead lungs. And now I wonder if she was watching a playback and seeing Dad rape her and seeing Mark sneak out from a vantage point at her bedroom window, watching him shrink away before her eyes, and I wonder if she knew what all this had done to us, and I wonder if she is reaching in and trying to move us, like the online map man, move us to another spot, a safer spot, or if she tried to move Dad before they met and wipe out me and Mark, like clearing the history on a computer.

And now I am walking and tears have dried on my face and I can feel the memory of them, tacky on my cheeks, like candyfloss. I look at myself and I want to move me to right now, because this playback is better than living. I am walking through an alleyway trying to find Mark. I know where the hostel is and as I bang on the door and I watch it open

slowly
and I see Mark with his top off
and track marks on his arms,
his hands,
his neck,
I wonder why I am telling him. I am telling him because I have no-one else and I remember this as I break the news, but I have to watch as he closes the door and I plan a funeral alone, and smile for aunts and uncles and cousins who didn't bother coming to see us as our lives disintegrated, yet visit now, eating sandwiches I had made with the ingredients I bought with some of the six hundred and fifteen pounds I found in the biscuit tin.

Then Mark walks back through the door of the house, which, post-probate, has no mortgage, it's our house, and I want to stop him but the solicitor says I can't. I try to fix him. I lock the doors and I tell him he can't go out to score. He screams at me, words I don't deserve and he kicks holes in the doors that belong to us. I patch them up and I lock them again. He breaks them. I fix them. He breaks them. He gets out one night and I lie on my bed, curled up like a baby. The biscuit tin money has nearly gone and I can't get a job because I need to be at home to stop Mark going out. I'm signing on and that covers the water bill arrears. I cry until my eyes are dry and then I sleep.

Sleep as well as you can but you know it's not ideal

you must be awake you must be alert

I wake up with a start and feel something in my face. **Where's the money,** what money, **the money Mum left you,** she didn't leave me any, **yes she did, you bitch, how have you been buying food and paying the bills and paying for wood to fix the doors?** There's fifty quid left, Mark, fifty quid, that's all we got, fifty quid, **give me the fifty quid,** get that gun away from me, where'd you get a gun anyway, **none of your business give me the money,** I can't, it's all we got, we got no more money and my giro won't come through for ten days and we need it and I haven't paid the bills, Mark, I can't pay the bills, we have to sell the house and no, I won't give you the money, I won't. And I see Mark moving away and the gun moves from my face and I sit up to watch him leave. I will barricade the door when he has gone. When he gets to the door he turns round and he smiles and I tentatively smile back and we will be ok, won't we, but...bang.

CHARLIE BROOKER KNEW

Charlie Brooker knew.

Don't like this post.

They look at the screen, at the boxes on the screen. Each box contains a face and each face exhibits a smile or a pout. Each face is static. There is no movement, no emotion. Some boxes have pictures of flowers, or food, or a car. These are the people who want to be their friends, but think they are not beautiful enough. Not beautiful enough to be virtually real.

Friends.

His girlfriend is in the room, but they have not had a conversation for days. They have said good morning what do you want for breakfast for lunch for dinner please hold the baby, but they have not spoken of feelings, or plans or physical life for days. They are shadows, sitting on opposite ends of the sofa, holding laptops, holding phones, holding tablets. Their baby gurgles whilst kicking toys and their cameras post evidence to the world. The baby grows bored and cries. Its parents sigh and type that they will be right back.

laugh out loud.

And when she flirts with a virtual friend of a friend, and when he finds it, he says nothing. The virtual world is everything but they can still pretend it means nothing.

De-friend

They sit next to each other, no tangible mood or excitement, no rolling on the floor laughing, like it used to be. They laugh with their virtual world and their virtual world laughs at them.

Follow

When they feel miserable, they tell the others, for hugs. They save lives of dogs and babies simply by liking horrific pictures; they feel no need to give to charity.

Like

Their shopping comes from this inter-world, using virtual cash. They choose clothes using a virtual model of themselves. They send soft pink light to people who feel sad.

Unlike

They watch life through a camera lens, then edit it to make it more beautiful. They smile together, but only because their friends will see. At the core of their lives sits a black box with blue, blinking lights. People will die but might not be missed in this virtual world.

Someone has implied that some people have forgotten there is a real world out there.

Subtweet

Unfollow

Nobody will like this post.

THE DAY YOU DIDN'T BLOW MY MIND

You say that moment by moment, it is rusting. Corroding something which corroded already, without my knowledge or permission. That insistence I have, insistence that every move is accounted, every minute counted, because without that, we can't fix. Metal can be hot, it burns before it damages and you have got to stop heating it, else it will change shape and become unrecognisable. The cogs of a relationship, they grind without trust, drip by drip I oil them, but your patience runs out too soon. Then what is left? Two parts of a machine which cannot work together, but are pointless apart. So where does it go, because something has to give? Either I forget, but not forget. I pretend, I keep it inside and I never mention how I broke. Or you let me feed the paranoia you planted and you let it live, then die, silently and without judgement. Or perhaps we move on and we forget, I forget, that I dreamt that one day you would marry me, despite our insistence that marriage is not for us. And forget the songs that play in our heads, and forget the Mondays and the Tuesdays and the days you blew my mind.

WALK A MILE

'Fucking immigrants. My country. Mine. It needs me, people like me. Not like them. You hear? MY birthplace, my heritage. Not theirs. I pay taxes. I pay your wages. And how about the fucking work-shy scum? Take their benefits away. The children, they will never amount to anything, anyway. Maintenance? Why should they pay maintenance? The mothers sit there, leeching money. They get the working tax credits, the men get nothing. Stop giving people houses, they'll soon find a job if you take away their roof. Take away their money. Depression? Ha! Pull your socks up, you miserable cunt. Pull your socks up, go to work, and then you'll know what depression is. I have a RIGHT to be angry, this is MY country. I'm going to take this to 10 Downing Street. Liberal, Labour. Do away with them. My country. They come here, they take our jobs, get given a house and a car and money. Money! Send them back to their own country...'

Yawning. I have been sleeping. My eyes are painful, as if someone has come in the night, scooped them out with a rusty spoon. I open my eyelids. It's an effort. I can't focus. Blinking, I stare at what should be the ceiling. It is different from the ceiling I stared at as I tried to sleep last night. Last night, when the anger coursed through my veins as I realised what a mess my country was in. Today, there is no anger. I feel fear. My arms are aching, tired with the weight of something heavy resting on them. I am cramped, but I can't stretch my legs. I can feel that I am moving, I am in a vehicle. I can smell rubber. I try to move my arms to rub my aching eyes, but I can't. They are trapped. I feel the vehicle stop. I hear a bang as a door closes. The bang is enough to remind me of gunfire, remind me that I have left my wife and children behind. Together, but alone. I am here to get a job, to raise money, to save them. I shuffle, trying to shift the weight on top of me. Something rolls away...a tyre. I am surrounded by tyres. Under me, on top of me, compressing me. I feel as if I am suffocating. I need to get out of here. I do not want this to be it. I do not want to die like this. I want to be a coward, to be caught, to be sent back home to hold my wife in my arms and kiss her, and tell her that everything will be alright, as long as we are together. We could all die together; better than dying alone. Coward. I must do this. I wriggle back under the mass that crushes my chest. My eyes try again to focus. They are not my eyes, I know this. They are not mine. My eyes had never before seen fear...

55

I can't see. I am tired. Eleven hours' sleep, yet I am still tired. Tired and pointless. Worthless. Ever wondered whether it is worth it? Existing, but not wanting to? Convincing yourself, each day, that life is not something to be terrified of; life is to be embraced. Life in an empty bed, an empty flat. An empty life. I look around and I see lights slowly forming blurred numbers. 08:22. What is the point? I may as well go back to sleep; there is nothing to get up for. I remember a time when I bounded from my bed at 06:35. Without fail, Monday through Friday. 08:15, on a weekend. I hated to waste the day, waste the sunshine, or the snow, or the angry wind. Invigorating. Put on my tie. Choose a different tie. Run with a cardboard cup of overpriced coffee. Banker. Now there is nothing. Lost my job, you see. Wife left me. Started drinking. Spiralling, down and down and down. Control. Out of control. No control. Kids don't want to see me. I don't want to be me. I have picked it up, slightly. Stopped drinking, started looking for a job. Any job. I want to see those kids, with their cheeky smiles. They used to love their Daddy. Shoulder-carries and days on the beach. A weight, but not the weight of the world. Card games, computer games, no mind games. Four cups, four plates, four forks. One cup, one plate, one fork. These are not my eyes, I know this. They are not mine. My eyes had never before seen desolation...

My eyes are streaming. There is something terribly wrong with them. What's that noise? It must still be early. I blink clear my tears and look at the clock. 5am. A bit early, even for my youngest child. I have four children, the oldest stay in bed till I wake them at 7 then hurry them along. Hurry them through breakfast, teeth-brushing, school-bag packing, kissing the hamster goodbye. Then I bundle my little family on the bus and drop them off at various places, so that I can go to Job Number 1. Job number 1 is 8am till 10am, filing pieces of paper in a factory. Orders and stuff. Car parts. Boss is a perv, looks at my tits, not my eyes. The tits that fed my kids, I sometimes remind him. Turns him on, I reckon. Job number 2 is 10.30am till midday. I pick up the phone in a dental surgery. Pick it up, listen, write stuff down, put it down, pick it up, listen, write stuff down, put it down. It's amazing how many phone calls you can rack up in ninety minutes. Then I become a midday supervisor at the primary school. Sometimes I see three of my four children, which makes me feel better. Job number 4 is in the evening. Whilst stirring a saucepan of pasta for the children's tea, I talk filth on the phone, for money. I sit the children in front of the television, the electronic babysitter, and I tell frustrated men that I want to suck them dry. For money. I want them to tie me up and fuck me till I scream. For money. I want them to piss on me, shit on me, whip me, force me, open me, hurt me. For money.

The children tell their father that they spend hours sitting on the floor, without me, whilst I chat on the phone. They can't know the truth. They can't know I do it for them, for money. Because their father loves them, you see. He loves them and he sees them, but he hates me, so he doesn't give me money. I have four jobs, and I have working tax credits. I have enough. So I hate myself, I punish myself. For them, for money. Looking in the mirror, I stare into my eyes. They are not my eyes, I know this. They are not mine. My eyes had never before seen desperation...

Running late. Fuck, I am running late. I have written it down, everything I have seen, and everything I have felt. I have walked miles in shoes of others. Now, again, I must walk in mine. Nodding to The Speaker of the House, I take my seat. I was right: my country needs me.

POWER

Behind the mask, you rule the world,
trembling, transient power
Corporation, gifted as
regret; a path I didn't mean to walk
Pretending, fallacious empathy
Appease my life, you cannot help
but sell
Platitudes are plentiful,
policies to protect
yourself.
Sell me to you:
you own me.
Sell my soul, or
keep me
enslaved
Covet more than you can steal
You need me more than I

DID ANYONE SEE?

The waves are rolling, lapping, cliched, like open mouths. Earlier that day she said that her brain felt too busy for her head; that she couldn't think of any particular one thing, and that entire thoughts seemed a lifetime ago. So she came to the beach to clear up the mess inside her, and now she's gone.

When he tells the police that of course it's not like her to do this, they look at each other with mirth playing around their mouths. Missing for three hours is not really missing, Sir, they say, not when your wife is thirty-five and of sound mind. She's a grown-up. Did you have an argument/is she trying to punish you/are you sleeping with anyone else/is she stressed/how is work for her?

He knows she wouldn't just go, and that, as far as he is concerned, missing for ten minutes is missing enough to be gone. She doesn't even leave the room without explaining why, and she said she would be home to eat the dinner he had made. And he's clutching her children's panic tightly against his chest and telling them she's probably gone to get chocolate bars as a surprise and, no, not dairy-free sugar-free stuff; real chocolate bars, the ones they like; the ones that ruin his diet.

But he's not kidding himself and he's not kidding them. She's not coming home and he doesn't know what to do anymore.

––––––––––––––

There isn't much he can do, other than pace, and so he paces. The children have gone to their rooms and he reckons they are plugged into social media because his calm has

neutralised their panic for now, but what he does not know, and will never know, is that they are staring open-mouthed at their walls and imagining life without their mum.

––––––––––––––

He asks the kids, the teens, where they think she will be, their mum. Because he knows that although he knows her, and thinks he knows her the best, she talks to the kids and holds them and calms them and has possibly said something to them. They reply – but why? she isn't hurt, is she? where is she? should we worry? what have you done? And he grasps at the panic in the air, and he catches it, and he holds it inside his head – twisting and turning and bucking and fighting like a caged animal – until the children, and his imagination, are silent again.

––––––––––––––

His biggest fear is being alone. The ringing of silence pokes at his ear drums, threatening to burst them.

––––––––––––––

Her biggest fear was being owned. To be hugged so tightly that she couldn't breathe.

––––––––––––––

His love for her is like that of an idol. Her pedestal is higher than he can reach and sometimes he gazes up at her as she stands there, better than him. She allows him to love
her and in return she throws him scraps: shreds of compliments, a smile at a joke, and she allowed him to save her from her former suitor, who had fathered her kids. His expectation was of picnics and football, of shiny cheeks and polite respect, but the kids prefer to listen, to watch, to stare at blue light than interact with any type of father figure, and his adoration of them bounces off their hearts.

––––––––––––––

She loves them – the teens – they look up to her but with love, not admiration. She would never leave them.

––––––––––––––

Did anyone see someone struggling with another human, grabbing and dragging and stifling? Did anyone see anyone, anything: think, think, think, DOES ANYONE KNOW WHERE SHE IS? She would not leave me. She simply would not.

––––––––––––––

Nothing is missing, except his wife. In psychological thrillers the police tell the husband to check to see if belongings have gone, because they are actors and they are acting like they care. In his life, this life, real life, the life in which his wife is missing, they didn't go as far as to act as though they care. But he checks anyway; he opens the door of the

wardrobe and he sees what he thinks is everything, but he can't be sure, how can anyone ever be sure? The crucial point in his investigation, his lonely investigation, is that she has gone but her kids are still here. As long as her kids are here he knows that she hasn't left him.

––––––––––––––

She's been gone for half a day now. Half a day, and what should he do? He wonders whether he could watch television, drink a whisky, walk around the town again. He wonders whether it is more appropriate to listen to sad songs on imperfect old vinyl instead. They don't show what to do in between the fear, the terror, the searching, when you watch the thrillers on BBC1. He tentatively knocks on the younger teen's door – she says come in and so he enters. It strikes him that she has been crying and he is frustrated that he can't help her feel better, but she has a wall in front of her face. He tells her it's ok, he adores her, he loves her like his own, but she doesn't respond. And he says she will be home soon, get some sleep, go to bed, sleep now, sleep even though your mother is missing, I am telling you, you have GCSEs in the morning. She says, yes, that is a good idea. He pats her lightly on the arm then his fingers close around her forearm just for a second, and she looks down at her phone and he leaves.

He knocks on the older teen's door but isn't invited in, and he wonders whether, if she never returns, he will manage to keep these teens in his life. He has been inside their

worlds for five years, long enough to warm to someone you'd think, but not long enough for the ice inside them to melt, it seems. He knocks again and a voice, a grunt, an affirmative gives him permission to open the door. He repeats the command to sleep then notices that the older teen doesn't have red eyes. The older teen shakes his head and also looks down at his phone, immersed in a text conversation. The teen rises from his position on the bed – he is growing taller by the day, and his slow unfurling is intimidating – and he says excuse me and walks past him and knocks on his sister's door. She says come in and it goes silent.

He is aware of privacy, but he doesn't give a shit as he tries to listen at the door like he usually does. Silence, other than the click click of phone keypads as though they are together but alone. Talking to each other with their mouths closed.

––––––––––––

He thinks that, in these situations, people print posters and leaflets and knock on doors to canvas the community. But he knows that the wireless printer doesn't want to be found either, so instead he walks to the corner shop and he asks them if they have seen her. The man knows him, he knows his wife, and he knows the teens. And he looks down and then up to the left and he says, no, I haven't. Can I get you some cigarettes? He replies no, thank you, as he wonders what the fuck is happening to his life. Thoughts like sharp pieces of a shattered glass pierce his mind. Let me breathe, she had said. Let me go. Let him go. Let her go. A familiar feeling is building inside him; he shudders as a shiver spreads from shoulder to shoulder and down his neck, and his heart pounds as it flips around in his chest cavity. His arms feel cold as goosebumps rise and he roars as he

realises what has happened. The man behind the counter shrinks and holds his back tightly against the cigarette display.

––––––––––––

As he walks home he hears a screech of tyres and he watches:

the teens getting into a car

her, at the wheel, still in her thinking clothes.

He watches, he sees, he knows, he knows, now he knows.

She doesn't need belongings, she doesn't need her wardrobe, her life he built for her. All she needs is her kids.

––––––––––––

As he walks the long length of the hallway he hears the piercing ringing of silence and loneliness and he wishes he could be at ease with it, he wishes he wasn't so afraid of being alone, of having nobody to control.

––––––––––––––

She fought, she won. Her head, which had been spinning, feels stable. She tests it. Thoughts are forming slowly, in entirety. Her kids are smiling, laughing, their eyes clear and no longer bound. They are free.

She is free.

THEATRE

'These violent delights have violent ends'
Shakespeare, Romeo and Juliet Act 2 Scene 6

MAKING A SCENE.

It was a village. A real one, not one of those crazy virtual global set-ups that mean nobody has to leave their house and use their legs and walk. No, this was the real deal. Villagers came and villagers went. Nodded at each other. Hugged and kissed and fucked and fought. Pushed each other over, while the others watched from their windows in their global village. Gladiatorial.

They probably didn't understand, in their glass houses, throwing stones. They heard snippets of another language, peppered with expletives. Fuck. Off. Now.

There are trees in the village; they get pissed on, crapped on. They survive and so there is no problem. But the spectators don't like to see this happening; they are sure that the village is designed for families:

small people, medium people and large people with picnics and multipacks of crisps. Not combatants, whatever their circumstances.

There was a fight one night. The spectators watched. Aghast yet with glee. When should we intervene, they wondered? When we see blood or death, or hear screams rather than blood-hungry howls? The spectators never physically fought; the windows and doors of their glass houses wouldn't take the weight of fighting bodies smashing against them. Their words, however, cut sharp like shattered glass.

And as they hold a glass of wine, they watch the combatants, the gladiators – the homeless and the drinkers – and they curse about the cursing, and they drink whilst they discuss the drinking and they swear that if they witness one more fight, they will punch the living daylights out of them.

The gladiators look up. Fucking wankers in their offices, in their homes, with their problems. What are they staring at? This isn't performance, this isn't theatre.

Gladiator One:

The future is yellow. Sorrows suppressed in my stomach, topped with swirling layers of super-strong lager, cider and the dregs of a bottle of tequila I found in the hand of a passed-out passer-by. It started off like this, and it will end like this. My parents drank, and the cycle cycled; I didn't break it. Couldn't break it. How can you break something so weak and flexible? It just bends and pings back to where it began. Wine was never water in my childhood home. The piss-yellow fluid lubricated the cogs of the cycle that would never cease. Luckily, I am the end. My sperm is ruined and there's no chance of anyone being born from that fruit. In my more lucid moments, that scares and saddens me. Makes me lie back on the bench, cans crackling and sharpening under my body, thinking about the what-ifs. But I know the end already; my future has been predicted.

Spectator One:

The future is yellow. Sorrows suppressed in my stomach, topped with swirling layers of Chablis, prosecco and the dregs of a glass of red I found in the back of the cupboard. It started off like this, and it will end like this. My mother drank, after my father left. My father drank before he left; couldn't stand the sight of my mother, or his kids. People speak of a cycle, but I'm not cycling; there doesn't have to be a reason, an excuse, when you have a home and a job and a beautiful wife and enough money to have the ingredients for your meals delivered in a neat little box every Tuesday. Boxes, money, piled high; high enough to hide the lies and the secrets. But, the gladiators, I'm not like them. I will never lubricate my secrets and mistakes with the dregs of a bottle of tequila I find in the hand of a passed-out passer-by.

––––––––––––––––––––––

Until now, you haven't known what this is about. This is about the people in the doorways, in the subways, on the steps of that neat little public garden, in the park, on the benches, in the bandstand, in the basement of the derelict house. The gladiators. It's about the people who watch them and judge them, and who are judged in return. The people who are judged for their perfect imperfect perfect lives. The spectators. They're all villagers. We're all villagers.

––––––––––––––––––––––

Gladiator One:

I focus on the double everything in front of me. My two-headed companion, with her blurry legs and smudged torso. She held my hand and my drink while I purged this morning's medication, and now she's taking a piss in the sea. I think I'm happy right now; I found a sleeping bag and the charity down the road gave me a tent. I pitched it on the beach. The thundering waves make it impossible to hear clearly, to think clearly. This, I think, is better than death. My gladiator companion is in the spotlight right now; she's taking her piss in the sea, staggering from foot to foot, peeling off her jeans to the soundtrack of tutting. We don't endear ourselves, I think. I wouldn't like her, pissing in the sea, if I didn't piss in the sea myself.

Spectator One:

I stare at her mouth and imagine the words she is saying appearing in tangible form. These words are brown and messy, dropping pieces of themselves at her feet, to be swept up at a later date. Disposable words that mean nothing. She is planning to subscribe to a monthly coffee plan. Two recyclable brown bags of the finest blend, posted into our lives on the 4th of each month. I've been dragged into this, thanks to the joint bank account.

We already have a recipe plan – little pots of herbs, but we have to buy the lamb. We have a meat plan – the lamb that goes with the herbs. We have a wine plan – the wine to go with the herbs and with the lamb. We have a cake plan – delivered monthly but we eat it in a week. What we don't have is a coffee plan. A fucking coffee plan. Yes. Let's get a coffee plan. We can drink coffee while listening to music from the music plan, or watching a film from the film plan. All the plans help to throw a blanket over the plan she wanted to get but was out of stock. The Baby Plan.

She's beautiful. A real stunner. Her beauty is so bright it gives me a headache, and sometimes I try to forget it. During these moments, I'll sit, head back and fingers steepled, fantasising about a different life; a simpler one. No plans, no nail varnish, no meals, no forgetting anniversaries, no her, no not wanting a baby. Just living. Off-grid. Me. Alone.

Cast away.

Gladiator One:

We fought last night, about the pissing in the sea. I imagine the little fish, weaver fish I think they're called, stinging people in revenge.

It's cold here, in the tent, on the beach. We were better off when we sat on the bench with the others. Someone brought along a radio one day; we danced to music in between the adverts. They were watching us and I drank some more because I might stink but I still get embarrassed.

I wonder what types of shape he throws, that guy at the window. He never smiles. He looks and I see him standing, watching me watching him. Who looked first?

I don't wonder how I got here because I know I wandered here. I saw the rich heading off the train and one day I followed. I wanted to understand the distance between us. I followed to a street in town that faces the sea, where the buildings groan under the pressure of perceived worth. Put the flats in a back alley and the pressure would be off. But, see, it's about the sea. About looking out of draughty windows, the breeze stinging your eyes and moving your hair, and watching the water behave and move its surroundings.

I set up home in a shelter outside a Victorian house. I'm far enough away not to hear the whispers but close enough to feel the daggers. The shelter has four sides and each side has a bench. Each bench faces a different direction, and each direction offers choice. North. South. East. West. Four climates in one day.

Spectator One:

There is one who looks up, as if he is worth looking down on. He looks up and then down into a can. Up and down in one swift move. He looks as though he wants to be there, living in scum, dancing with the girl who pisses everywhere. One day they had some sort of rave: music punctuated by drinking, dancing punctuated by drinking, drinking punctuated by nothing.

She came home, upset, stinking of another guy. I'm not jealous but I am easily offended. He's probably not even her type; the stench hanging off her clothes is supermarket deodorant, probably 3 for 2. She shags him just to try to get a kid, and then what? She thinks I don't know that she plans to pass the kid off as mine; I have money, a flat, a life I built with her encased in it, like when a biscuit crumb gets trapped under sticky tape.

I still think I should leave, but I've spent so much time and effort and money on these walls; on this existence. I've perfected habits, suppressed urges. I feel I've swum a million miles from myself, from what I am. Who am I to take this guy, this imperfect clone, from the life I have built for him?

I know when this happened. It happened while I was hurting. While my life was corroding. All those years ago; years which changed me. Years during which he cheated on me. Him. I loved him.

Gladiator One:

Waking up, inhaling stench, scratching at the welts left by the fake wool blanket, sleeping on a hard bench, ketones on my breath, feet cornflake-crusted and dry and bare – I'm only 6-foot-tall because of the hard skin underneath. And how I laugh at that as I prise open my eyes with the only strength I can muster and I remember, yes, I remember; everything I can and I know that perhaps it all needs to change.

Clicking shoes down the corridor outside and the metal door shakes as the hatch drops, but there's a second before a face appears and I want to tell the face that it shouldn't be scared, it shouldn't have to step to one side in case a fist appears through the hatch. Nobody should have to feel fear. Fear is the worst of all emotion.

I agree that yes, they should take my fingerprints in

case I am assuming a false identity, and the face's eyes roll as she takes the prints because she knows it's me; I always ask for a lasagne and a blanket and a cup of cold orange squash. And I wait as the prints are processed and the machine agrees that yes, it is me, and another machine adds a photo to my file and some important fingertips type that I am fit to be released into the wild and a voice tells me that if I get drunk in a public place again I am likely to be looking at fear in faces and metal doors for a year.

Spectator One:

Watched him drinking, stumbling into flower beds as I stumble against walls. I saw his face for the first time, in reality. There was dirt smudged on his face from the flowers, and there was a beard and blue eyes. And I stood on the balcony and watched as his body defied the poison inside, holding him almost upright despite the shit coursing through his veins and I closed my eyes and swayed to the beat of my heart.

A cigarette butt between his lips lit by a passer-by and at that moment I wished I was him. I wished my life would fuck off with her pedicures and nail stickers and heaters for this and that and gizmos that made her pretty. And I wished again for the light caressing touch of no responsibility, even if it meant tough nights on hard benches. And I imagined the touch I felt before I was cheated on, the touch that I thought would electrify my nerves forever. And I am angered that I am here, that I will end up always here, that the Chablis will keep pouring into my mouth and the subscriptions will keep dropping through my letterbox and that my wife will keep wanting-not-wanting me. And I am furious, and the world turns red and I scream and I turn and I find my phone and with drunken fingers I call the police and I tell them all about that man who is sleeping amongst the flowers.

Gladiator One:

A support worker visited me today. You see, I'd told the police that I had moved from the tent on the beach because I couldn't bear to spend all my time with the girl who pisses in the sea. I now live on the most-sheltered northern bench of the shelter, the others scattered around me like corpses. The police sent the support worker. She is nice, smells of flowers but has probably never googled the ingredients in the shower gel to see whether the plastic beads that make her skin so soft will ruin our earth.

Her hair is being whipped east and west, getting trapped on her lip gloss during its journey. She keeps hooking her little finger under strands and easing them away, rubbing her lips together to remove the gloss. She is getting pissed off with this, I can tell. She wants to know my story, and I tell her it will bore her. She laughs a little, but it's not real. She sits a metre from me as though I am catching, or I will lurch or leap into her and change her life.

I tell her that I was in care, but they did not care. That I cared so little that I left care, and that care never followed me. I tell her that I do care now, but just for myself. That I want to sleep on the southern bench. That I have a companion who looks after me in the only way she knows how, that she turns up just after the shops open with cheap own-brand lager and a handful of fag butts. Sometimes she brings cigarette papers and we scratch the blackened tobacco off the top of the butts and roll the dry brown stuff, making brand new throat-catching head-spinning roll-ups. I tell her that I like the thought and the love that goes into this mess, but that in the day I want to watch the sea through clear eyes, but that the girl who pisses in the sea, her kindness holds me paralysed on the wrong side of the shelter. And that although the others are scattered around me and the drink I consume interacts with them; it fights them and shouts at them; I don't even know their names and I am not like them. I tell her that the outdoors suits me and that the sometimes-cold-and-rain is a suitable punishment to atone for those I steal from, or those I have mugged or robbed or shouted at or used or passively annoyed along the way. And I don't mind that because even if I was inside a glass house I would still atone somehow. I would clean dirty bins or filthy windows, or I would wash up forks with ground-on food, or I would have to put washing away or live with someone annoying or noisy. Maybe the girl who pisses in the sea. So, yes, I am happy here. But I am not happy with the need, with the urge, with the abuse, the misuse, the mistakes, the blurred vision or with the judgement.

And I sense something happening around me and I think I see a carrot fly by and then I wonder if I have drunk too much, or even not enough, and I shrug and I move on.

And the kind lady opens her rucksack and passes me a bottle of water, a packet of fags and a copy of Romeo and Juliet that she found on the train.

And that guy, the one who watches, he fell in front of me and I said you ok, I'm ok he said, but I could feel the silence between our words dragging, heavy with something else.

Spectator One:

He's got a visitor; I watch her arrive. I watch her get out of her car and take her first tentative step towards the bench, inhaling a deep breath and straightening her neck, her back. I can tell she is nervous and that the books she read and the presentations she watched did not prepare her for the reality of getting out of her car and approaching an unwashed man on an unwashed bench.

My wife is home late today. I know this because I

have to take delivery of her organic seasonal fruit and veg box. All seasonal means is that she changes her preferred smoothie flavour four times a year. When I asked her if you could smoothie a TURNIP she muttered that if she had thought things through properly she would have opted for poor and happy instead.

I express surprise that she is so late and she shouts that she is ALLOWED to come home WHENEVER she likes and that perhaps I should stop TIMING her she tells me to FUCK OFF, but she fucks off instead and forgets to take her fucking sweet potatoes with her.

And I'm not proud of this but I wait until she is under the balcony and one by one by one I throw her fucking stupid vegetables at her and she dances a dance of falling potatoes carrots apples and cabbage and then she shouts that I am a cunt and walks on by.

And when she has gone I look past the potatoes back to the bench and I see that the lady is sitting far enough from him to ensure he won't brush against her and as I watch I see her shoulders relax and I see a smile play on his lips, and I smile too and I stop to wonder why. Then I see her pass him some water and a packet of cigarettes and a book and I wonder what the book is. Probably drivel about empowerment and mindfulness and breathing properly and taking time to listen to the screaming inside.

I need to see what he is reading, to add it to my list of disdain. I grab my coat and my keys and I descend the

stairs and steps and slopes into his world. He is reading the book with the cover facing the pavement so I
need to be smaller; I bend to pretend to tie my shoe-
laces and as I bend the whisky travels to my knees,
weakening them. I look up as I stumble and see his
eyes and Romeo and Juliet and I can feel myself tum-
bling into his life.

Gladiator One:

He's there, in front of me and in my mind, simultan-
eously inhabiting both with a presence that is more
real than my own self. My mind whirs and falls with
him and I watch as he looks up. And as he looks up I
piece together what is real and what isn't, and I real-
ise that his eyes have caught mine, I did not imagine
that. And although I cannot usually focus; my pupils
bouncing from side to side to side; in that moment,
that one moment, the world stops spinning and
bouncing just for a second. And a shrill voice pierces
the stillness of my non-spinning world, and in enters
the girl who pisses in the sea, stage left.

She puts her hand on my shoulder and she says, who
the fuck are you, to the guy who is always watching
me. And I always imagined this confident spectator
to win a conversation but this one he loses. He mumbles something and he gathers and unfolds unstead-
ily to his feet, but his eyes, they never unlock from
mine, I feel excitement rise from my stomach to my
throat, constricting it like gentle hands, and when

the feeling moves on and up it begins to squeeze the top of my nose and then it is behind my eyes, my non-spinning eyes, making them prickle and sting as though he is moving within them, adjusting my focus, adding thoughts I have never before contemplated or even begun to try to understand.

Spectator One:

His pupils constrict and expand as though a light is turning on and off and on and off; as though he can't make up his mind. As I watch he blinks and his pupils dilate again and I am so close that I can see my face in their black black depths. I'm not sure what is happening but suddenly my stomach is constricting and my bowels feel loose and all I can think is that I need to sit down or stand up before something gives way or plummets through me. Reality pierces my earholes as the girl who pisses in the sea asks who the fuck are you and I can't reply; I cannot remember; my name is inconsequential. So I put my hands flat beside my feet, easing my weight upwards, and I unfold to a standing position, carefully, and I brush down my trousers and I say, have a nice day, and I walk back up the slopes, back up the steps, back up the stairs, back to my podium.

I close the door behind me and lean, bending my weak knees until I am crouching, not like a predator but like frightened prey, and I hear a fumbling and the sharp sound of a key trying to find a lock and oh god oh god oh fucking hell she's back.

This time she has been to the shopping centre and she has bought a stick and in the toilets in the shopping centre she has pissed on it. And while I was falling into a heap on the pavement outside my life, her life was just beginning. Her life began with two lines.

The weakness inside me takes over from any strength I have forced myself to grow, and it pushes through my skin and coats me in a clinging beige film. And I can feel it suffocating me; emanating; layering on top of the lies on my skin. The weakness is me, and the weakness stands me up on my wobbling legs and it straightens my arm and my wrist and my fingers and with my fingers it touches her shoulder. It forms words with my mouth and the words it forms are I am sorry, and then it helps me open the door and on the wobbling legs, weakness walks me away from my life.

Gladiator One:

I shake my shoulder until her hand stops touching and I stare at the door that swallowed him. The others are white noise in the background. The air is too still and I know my life is about to change. I see his wife walk through the door that swallowed him.

I want him.

I walk towards the door that swallowed him, but it opens before I can reach it, and he staggers out. He has nothing but his keys, and I know, he knows, we know, that he won't be needing them again.

I hold his gaze and he walks towards me; later, through gasping breaths, he tells me that this was the moment in which he knew he needed nothing.

I can feel my companion's eyes boring into the back of me and somewhere, on another plane, I hear something smashing. I hear mumbles and chattering and JUST TRY TO STOP ME

Spectator One:

His eyes so blue, searching me

But something else is happening, behind him, behind me

The girl who pisses in the sea is wielding a bottle, smashed

The others holding her back

But there is something else

Gladiator One:

His eyes focus behind me; mine don't focus behind him, and I turn to see my companion wielding a bottle ready to fight me, to fight him.

But then I hear a gurgling noise and I turn again to see his wife pull the knife out from his back as expressions fight each other for room on their faces and I still can't comprehend what has happened.

She runs, her feet stamping a path

He does nothing

I move towards him

Touching his sticky back

Forcing the blood back inside, back inside so it can be caught and pumped to send some colour back to his ashen face

I need nothing, he says

Leaning in, I tell him that I wish it had been different; that instead of watching I had done something. And for the first time in my life I learn from my mistakes, for in that moment, instead of not doing something, I kiss him as he dies.

'Thus with a kiss I die'

Shakespeare, Romeo and Juliet Act 5 Scene 3

Untouched by fault,
a little, but enough.

Be false,

yet be true;

a belying touch.

It's never said;

does it live inside?

Write it, feel it,

speak it

I don't mind.

Fin

THANK YOU

Awesome reader, thank you, thank you, thank you. Your support means the absolute world to me; please continue to shop small and support indie. Check out authorkarinaevans.com for your free Volcano excerpt.

PS. Please leave a review; how else would anyone to know what to buy?

ABOUT THE AUTHOR

Karina Evans

Author and mother-of-three from Hastings, East Sussex; Karina's works focus primarily on social issues, including homelessness, domestic violence and substance misuse.

BOOKS BY THIS AUTHOR

Volcano

It is the 22nd of July, 2001. Eloise Katherine Bennett, a devoted mother of two, has died after falling down the stairs at her home. On the face of it, Eloise led an unenviable life. Her husband, Paul, was a violent bully, and her mother, Sandra, a control freak. Eloise and her children suffered at their uncompromising hands for many years. . Via flashbacks and through the voices of Eloise and those who have influenced her in life, we learn the truth behind her death. Live. Love. Leave. Life. Death. A story of vulnerability, in even the hardest of hearts.

Printed in Poland
by Amazon Fulfillment
Poland Sp. z o.o., Wrocław

59165182R00059